Dear Parents:

Congratulations! Your child is taking the first steps on an exciting journey. The destination? Independent reading!

STEP INTO READING® will help your child get there. The program offers five steps to reading success. Each step includes fun stories and colorful art or photographs. In addition to original fiction and books with favorite characters, there are Step into Reading Non-Fiction Readers, Phonics Readers and Boxed Sets, Sticker Readers, and Comic Readers—a complete literacy program with something to interest every child.

Learning to Read, Step by Step!

Ready to Read   **Preschool–Kindergarten**
• big type and easy words • rhyme and rhythm • picture clues
For children who know the alphabet and are eager to begin reading.

Reading with Help   **Preschool–Grade 1**
• basic vocabulary • short sentences • simple stories
For children who recognize familiar words and sound out new words with help.

Reading on Your Own   **Grades 1–3**
• engaging characters • easy-to-follow plots • popular topics
For children who are ready to read on their own.

Reading Paragraphs   **Grades 2–3**
• challenging vocabulary • short paragraphs • exciting stories
For newly independent readers who read simple sentences with confidence.

Ready for Chapters   **Grades 2–4**
• chapters • longer paragraphs • full-color art
For children who want to take the plunge into chapter books but still like colorful pictures.

STEP INTO READING® is designed to give every child a successful reading experience. The grade levels are only guides; children will progress through the steps at their own speed, developing confidence in their reading.

Remember, a lifetime love of reading starts with a

Five
Classic
Tales

Visit us on the Web!
StepIntoReading.com
randomhouse.com/kids

Educators and librarians, for a variety of teaching tools, visit us at RHTeachersLibrarians.com

ISBN 978-0-7364-3180-4

MANUFACTURED IN CHINA   10 9 8 7 6 5 4 3 2

STEP INTO READING®

Five Classic Tales

Step 1 and 2 Books

A Collection of Five Early Readers

Random House 🏠 New York

Contents

DUMBO

Fly, Dumbo, Fly!

By Jennifer Liberts Weinberg

Illustrated by Carlo LoRaso and John Kurtz

Random House New York

Peekaboo.

Who are you?

Dumbo!

"Achoo!"

Oh, dear.
Big ears.

A parade!

Oh, dear.

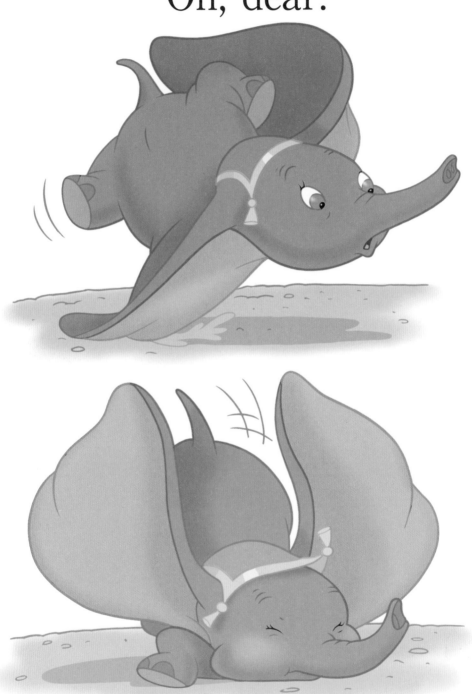

Those ears!

Poor Dumbo.

Who is there?

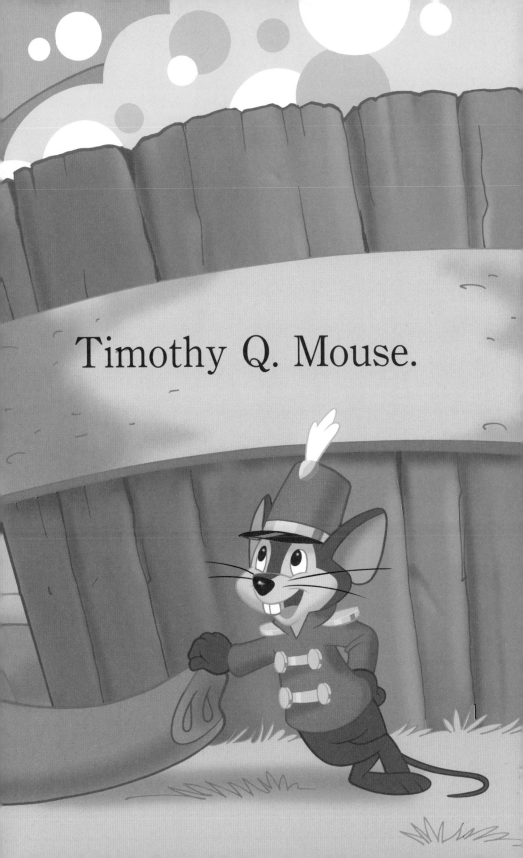

Timothy Q. Mouse.

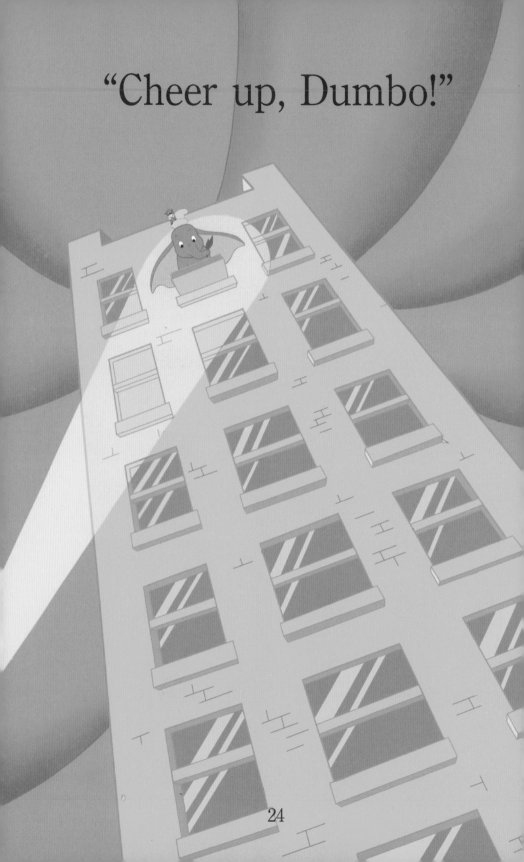

"Cheer up, Dumbo!"

Friends!

Dumbo tries.

Dumbo trips!

Wings!

"Jump, Dumbo!"

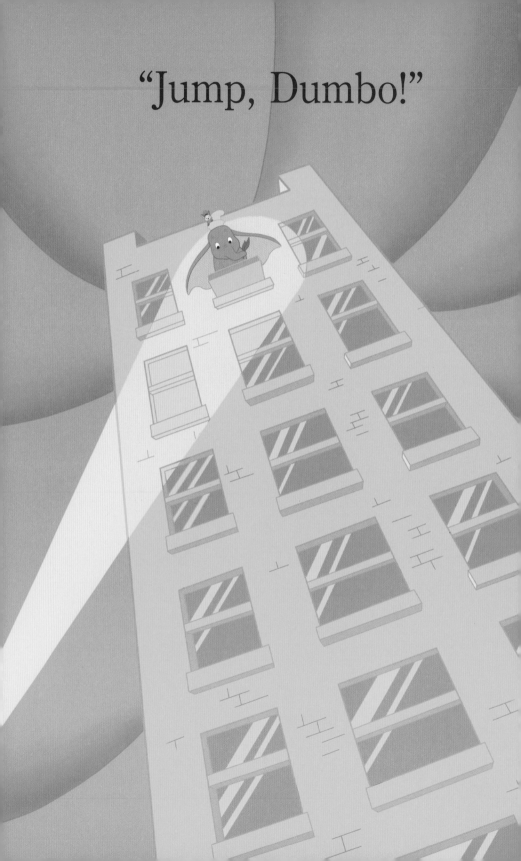

Down, down, down.

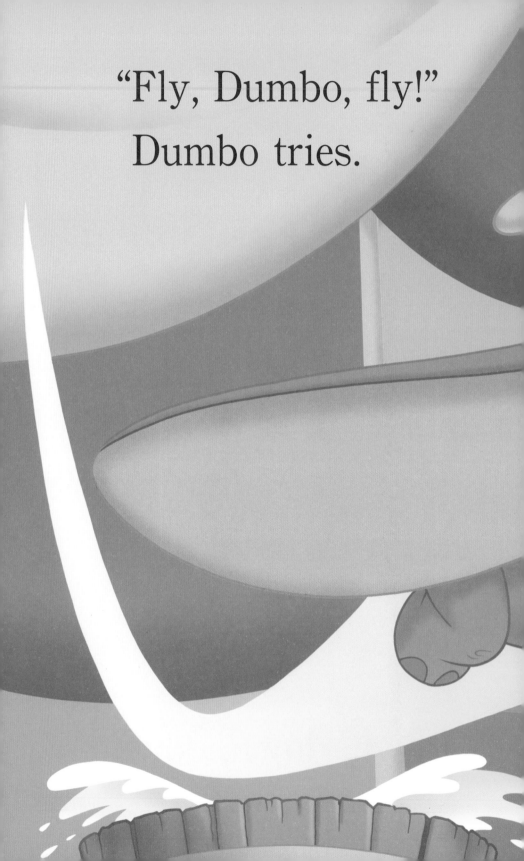

"Fly, Dumbo, fly!"
Dumbo tries.

Up, up, up.
Dumbo flies!

Loop-the-loop!

"Way to go, Dumbo!"

Peter Pan

Adapted by Christy Webster
Illustrated by the Disney Storybook Artists

Random House New York

Bedtime.

Peter Pan!

Fairy dust.

They can fly!

Fly to Never Land!

Meet Tinker Bell.

Follow the Lost Boys.

See mermaids.

Pirates!

Oh, no!

Captain Hook's ship.

Walk the plank.

Saved!

Brave Peter.

Clumsy Captain!

Take the ship!

Fly home.

Bedtime.

DISNEY

Bambi

Bambi's
Hide-and-Seek

By Andrea Posner-Sanchez

Illustrated by Isidre Monés

Random House New York

Bambi.

Thumper.

Hide-and-seek!

Counting.

Hiding.

Is that Thumper
behind the bush?

That is not Thumper!

"Shh!"

Inside the tree?

Nuts!

That is not Thumper!

In the creek?

That is not Thumper!

"Ribbit!"

By the log?

Tap, tap, tap.

"You are not Thumper!"
says Bambi.

Bambi rests.

"Achoo!"

There is Thumper!

"Let's play again!"

DISNEY

Lady and the TRAMP

Adapted by Delphine Finnegan

Illustrated by the Disney Storybook Artists

Random House 🏠 New York

Christmas morning,
Jim Dear gave Darling
a surprise.
She opened the gift box.
A pretty new puppy
popped out.
Jim Dear and Darling
called her Lady.

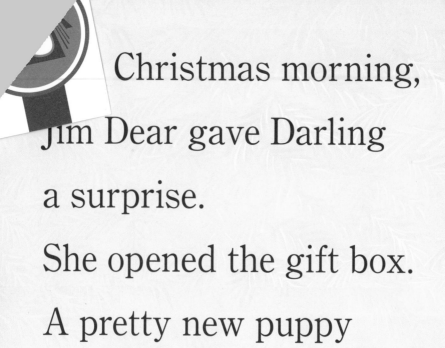

Lady watched
over the house.
She took care
of everyone—
even the fish.

Lady had good friends.

She had a great life.

Then Jim Dear
and Darling
had a baby.

Lady was happy.
She would take care
of the baby, too.

A few months later,
Jim Dear and Darling
took a trip.
Aunt Sarah came
to watch the baby.
She had many bags.

Two cats popped out
of one bag.
They surprised Lady.

The cats made a mess.

Lady stopped them.

Aunt Sarah thought

Lady had made the mess.

"Bad dog,"

said Aunt Sarah.

She made Lady

wear a muzzle.

Lady ran away.

Mean dogs chased her.

Tramp was a nice dog.

He was a stray.

He did not have a home.

Tramp liked
to help other dogs.

He would help Lady.

Tramp snarled.

He bared his teeth.

The mean dogs ran away.

Tramp saved Lady.

Next,
Tramp led Lady
to the zoo.

At the zoo,

a beaver chewed

through the muzzle.

Lady was free!

Tramp took Lady
to dinner.
They ate spaghetti
and meatballs.

The chefs sang songs.

It was a beautiful night.

Lady and Tramp

fell in love.

When Lady went home,
she had to stay outside.
Aunt Sarah
tied her to a chain.

No one could
cheer Lady up.

That night,

Lady saw a rat.

The rat climbed

into the baby's bedroom.

Lady barked and barked.

Aunt Sarah woke up.

"Be quiet,"

she said.

Tramp heard Lady, too.

He wanted to help.

He ran into the house.

He snarled and snapped

at the rat.

Lady was still scared.

She had to take care

of the baby.

She broke her chain.

Tramp caught the rat.

The baby was safe.

Lady and Tramp
made a great team.

Now it was Lady's turn
to help Tramp.
Jim Dear and Darling
came home that night.

Lady showed them how
Tramp had helped her.
Tramp had a new home!

The next Christmas,
the family grew.
Lady loved taking care
of the baby, Tramp,
and her puppies.

STEP INTO READING®

STEP 2

Disney

ALICE in WONDERLAND

Adapted by Pamela Bobowicz

Illustrated by the Disney Storybook Artists

Random House 🏠 New York

Alice was a young girl.
She liked to daydream.
She dreamed
of a strange land.
She wanted to go there.

A white rabbit ran by.
He looked at
his pocket watch.

"I'm late!"

he cried.

Alice ran after him.

The rabbit went
under a tree.

He went down a hole.

Alice followed.

She fell

down, down, down.

Alice was in

a strange forest.

She followed
the rabbit
to his house.

Alice went
into the house.
She ate some cookies.

The cookies made her
grow and grow.
She grew too big
for the house!

A dodo bird
gave her a carrot.
She ate the carrot.
It made her shrink!

Now Alice was smaller
than the bird.
The White Rabbit
ran away.

Alice searched for

the rabbit again.

She met some flowers.

They could talk!

They asked her what

kind of flower she was.

"I'm a girl, not a flower,"
Alice told them.

The flowers laughed.

Alice ran away.

Next Alice met
the Mad Hatter
and the March Hare.

They were having

a tea party.

The Mad Hatter
had a cake.
It was
under his hat!

He let Alice
make a wish.
She wished to find
the White Rabbit.

Alice was tired.
She could not find
the White Rabbit.
No one could help her.

Then Alice met a cat.

"I'm lost,"

she told him.

The cat asked Alice
where she wanted to go.
Alice didn't know.
"Then you're not lost!"
the cat said.

The cat led Alice

to a castle garden.

The White Rabbit
was there!
He worked for
the Queen of Hearts.

Alice wanted
to go home.
She told the Queen.

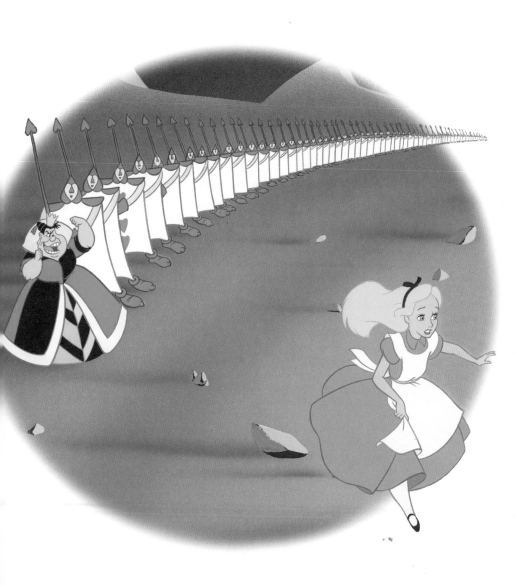

The Queen was angry.

Alice ran away.

Alice heard
her cat purring.
She opened her eyes.
She was home again.
It had all been a dream!